First U.S. Edition

First published in Great Britain by Frances Lincoln Limited, 4 Torriano Mews, Torriano Avenue, London NW5 2RZ

ISBN 0-316-80466-5

Library of Congress Catalog Card Number 94-76697

10 9 8 7 6 5 4 3 2 1

Published simultaneously in Canada by Little, Brown & Company (Canada) Limited

Printed in Hong Kong

THE LEOPARD'S DRUM

With thanks to Amoafi Kwapong and Peter Sarpong

Jessica Souhami

THE LEOPARD'S DRUM

An Asante Tale from West Africa

Little, Brown and Company
Boston New York Toronto London

Osebo, the leopard, was fierce, proud, and boastful.
He made a huge drum, and he played it every day.

Animals came from near and far to see it. It was
a magnificent drum, the best they had ever seen.
They all wished it belonged to them.

Even Nyame, the Sky-God, wanted it.

"Osebo," he said, "that's a wonderful drum. *I* should have a drum like that. Will you give me your drum?"

"No," said Osebo.

"Will you lend me your drum?"

"No!" said Osebo.

"Will you let me try your drum?"
But Osebo said, "NO!"
"You should respect me, Osebo. I am the Sky-God."
Then Nyame turned and said, "Animals of the forest,
whoever brings me that drum will get a big reward."
And Nyame disappeared.

The next day, Onini, the python, went to get
the drum.

"Looking for me, Onini?"
"Oh, er—no, Osebo. . . .
Just looking at your fine drum,
your huge drum,
your magnificent drum. . . .
Good-day Osebo."

The next day, Esono, the elephant, went to get the drum.

"Looking for me, Esono?"
"Oh, er—no, Osebo.
Just admiring your fine drum,
your huge drum,
your magnificent drum, Osebo.
Good-bye, Osebo."

The next day,
something strange
moved slowly through
the forest.

The animals were puzzled.
Some were frightenend.
"What is it?" they whispered.
"Whoever can it be?"

It was Asroboa, the monkey,
going to get the drum.
He hoped Osebo wouldn't see him
behind his mask.

"Looking for me, Asroboa?"
"Ohhh, no, Osebo.
Just looking . . . fine . . . huge . . .
mag . . . ni . . . fi . . . cen . . . t."

Last of all Achi-cheri, the tortoise,
went to get Osebo's drum.
"You haven't got a chance,"
the other animals said, "not a titchy little,
weak little creature like you!"

It was true, the tortoise was very small, and in those days her shell was quite soft. She had to watch out that careless animals didn't squash her flat.

"Well, I'm going to try anyway," she said.

"Looking for me, Achi-cheri?"

"Not really, Osebo. I was just looking at this drum."

"Don't you think it's a fine, magnificent drum, Achi-cheri?"

"Well, it's all right, I suppose, for a middle-sized kind of drum, Osebo."

"*Middle-sized*? You ridiculous creature, don't you know this is the biggest, the best drum in the forest?"

"Well," said Achi-cheri, "I've heard that Nyame's got a bigger drum."

"What!" said Osebo.

"Oh, yes. It's so big, he can climb right inside it and not one bit of him sticks out."

"Well, I can climb right inside mine," said Osebo. "Just watch."

Osebo began to squeeze himself into the drum.

"Am I inside, Achi-cheri?"

"No, not nearly, Osebo."

"Now, Achi-cheri?"

"No, not quite, Osebo."

"Now, Achi-cheri?"

"Yes, Osebo, now you're inside. But you can't get out!"
And Achi-cheri sealed the drum with a large cooking pot.
"Now I'm going to take you to the Sky-God."

Slowly, Achi-cheri pushed the enormous drum with the
heavy leopard inside it all the way to Nyame.

"Here is Osebo's drum, Nyame. And Osebo is inside."

"Well done!" said Nyame. "No one else could get the drum. And you have taught that boastful leopard a lesson. Let him go now, and decide what you would like as your reward."

Achi-cheri looked around. All the other animals were looking jealous and annoyed. She thought for a moment.

"Please, Nyame," she said, "most of all I would like a hard shell to protect me from fierce animals."

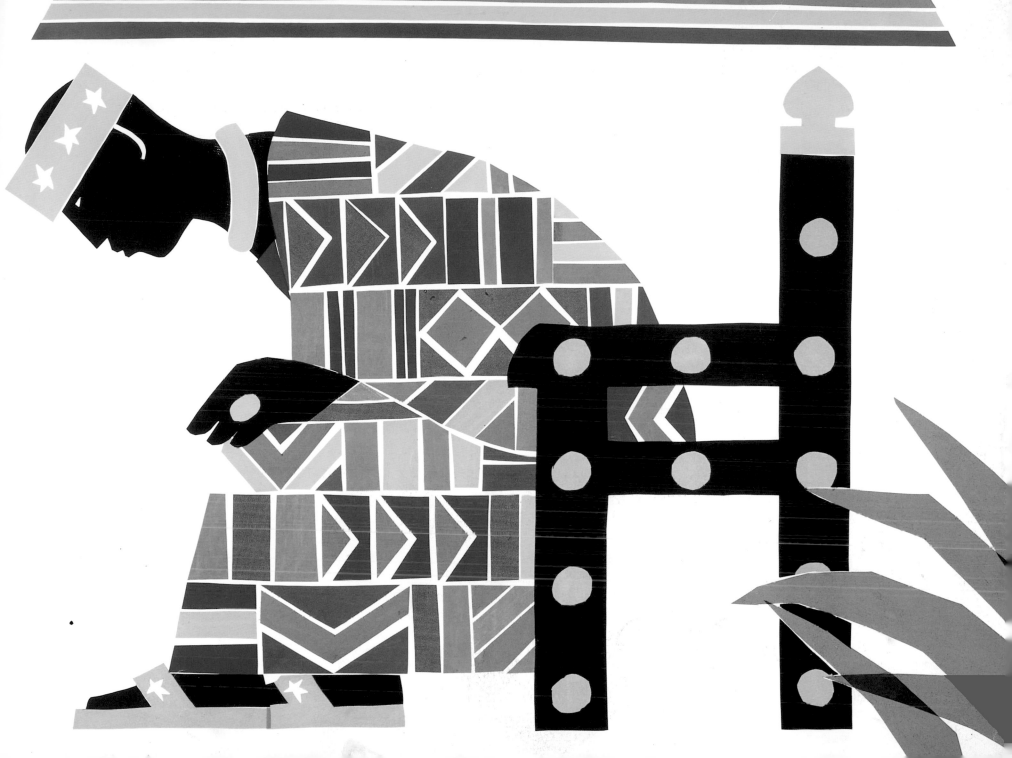

Nyame laughed and gave her a tough, hard shell.
And Achi-cheri, the tortoise, still wears it today.